BRITISH VALUES

WHO DID THAT?

SASHA LEARNS ABOUT RESPONSIBILITY

WRITTEN BY DEBORAH CHANCELLOR

ILLUSTRATED BY ELIF BALTA PARKS

W

FRANKLIN WATTS

LONDON • SYDNEY

KU-675-914

...ts County Library
Leabharlann Chontae Laoise

Acc. No. 18/2890

Class No. ...... JF

... No. 14865

Sasha was playing football in the garden.
Her little brother wanted to play, too.

"Pass me the ball," Sasha said to Henry.
"Then I'll score a fantastic goal!"

CRASH!

Sasha kicked the ball at a window.

Dad ran into the garden.

"WHO DID THAT?" Dad yelled.
Sasha didn't want to get told off.
"It wasn't me!" she said.

Sasha pointed to her brother.
"It was him!" she said.

Dad was angry with Henry.
"Go to your room!" he said.

Henry was upset.

He was cross with Sasha and Dad.

"I'm not staying here!" he said.
"I'm going to run away."

Henry sneaked out of the house.
He went to see Grandma.

"What happened, sweetie?" she asked.
"You can tell me all about it."

Back at home, Sasha felt guilty.
She decided to tell Dad the truth.

Dad was not happy with Sasha.
"We must both say sorry
to Henry," he said.

Sasha and Dad looked for Henry.
They couldn't find him anywhere.
Dad was very worried.

"Perhaps Grandma will know
where Henry is," Sasha said.

They went to Grandma's house.
"Is Henry here?" Dad asked Grandma.

"He ran away and it's all my fault!" Sasha said.
Then she burst into tears.

Henry appeared at the door.
"I'm really sorry!" Sasha cried.

"Me too," said Dad.
"Let me take you to the park."

Sasha stayed behind with Grandma.
Grandma gave her a hug.

"Don't let someone else pay
for your mistakes," Grandma said.
"It's better to own up
and take the blame."

Sasha and Grandma went to find
Henry and Dad in the park. Henry was
eating a huge ice cream.

"Come and share this with me," Henry said to Sasha. "Then let's play football again!"

- Can you tell Sasha's story?

- Why didn't Sasha own up to what she did?

- Why did Henry run away from home?

- What did Sasha and Dad have to do to sort things out?

3.

4.

5.

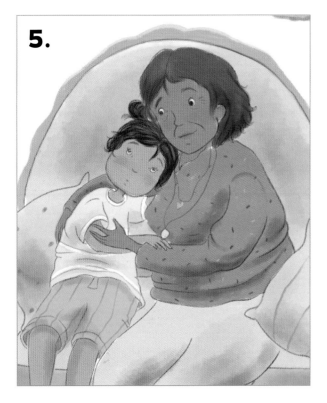

6.

A note about sharing this book

The 'British Values' series provides a starting point for further discussion on universal principles in society, such as tolerance, respect and responsibility. The values and ethics considered in each book are relevant to all, children and adults alike.

Who Did That?

This story explores, in a familiar context, some issues surrounding responsibility. It demonstrates key concepts on this theme, such as the importance of owning up to our mistakes, rather than blaming others for them. Mistakes often have consequences but these are made worse if we don't admit to the mistakes in the first place. In this story, Sasha breaks a window and blames it on her brother Henry – he is so upset he runs away from home. The original mistake, or accident, is not as serious as what happens when Sasha refuses to take responsibility for it. *Who Did That?* encourages the reader to conclude, with Grandma, that it is always better to own up when we do something wrong, even if we didn't mean to do it in the first place. This is a cautionary tale with an important message, which can be applied to many everyday situations.

The wordless storyboard on pages 26 and 27 gives the opportunity to practise speaking and listening skills. Children are encouraged to retell the story illustrated in the panels.

How to use the book

The story is designed for adults to share with either an individual child or a group of children, and as a starting point for discussion. The book provides visual support to build confidence in children who are starting to read on their own. The story introduces vocabulary that is relevant to the theme of responsibility, such as: 'told off', 'pointed', 'guilty', 'truth', 'sorry', 'fault', 'mistake', 'own up', 'blame'.

Who Did That? is told from Sasha's point of view, but it would be interesting to hear the same story from a different perspective. Ask the children to tell the story, imagining they are Henry, and that Sasha is their big sister. Retelling the story from Henry's point of view will help children to empathise with how he feels about being blamed for something he didn't do.

Before reading the story

Pick a time to read when you and the children are relaxed and can take time to share the story together. Before you start reading, look at the illustrations and discuss what the book may be about.

After reading, talk about the book with the children:

- What is the story about? What does Sasha do and why doesn't she own up?
- Why is Henry angry? Whose fault is it that Henry runs away and why? What does Sasha have to do to make things better? Should Dad punish Sasha for what she did? What is worse – smashing the window or blaming Henry?
- Invite the children to talk about a time when they didn't take responsibility for something they did wrong. What happened? How did this make them feel? Would they do the same thing again?
- Talk a bit more about responsibility, and what the word means. When we are responsible for something, people rely on us to do that thing. Discuss the kinds of things people are responsible for. Different people have different responsibilities, for example, parents and teachers are responsible for the safety and care of children. What sort of things are children responsible for? Most children are responsible for looking after their toys, and possibly pets.
- Talk about what happens when people do not take responsibility for their actions. In this story, Sasha lies to her dad and upsets her brother. Do the children think she should be punished for this? Why, or why not?
- Look at the end of the story again. When Sasha talks with Grandma about what happened, she feels bad. Talking about her problem helps her feel better. At the end of the story, Henry forgives Sasha, and plays with her again. For things to improve, it is necessary for Sasha to talk about her problem, say sorry, and for Henry to forgive her for what happened. Talk about the importance of finding a resolution to problems, so that everyone can move on from them.
- Look at the wordless storyboard. Ask the children to talk about Sasha's feelings as the story develops. What does she learn from her experience? How would the children feel, if they were in Sasha's position? What did the children learn from this story?

Franklin Watts
First published in Great Britain in 2017 by The Watts Publishing Group

Copyright © Franklin Watts, 2017

All rights reserved.

Credits
Series Editor: Sarah Peutrill
Series Designer: Cathryn Gilbert

Every attempt has been made to clear copyright.
Should there be any inadvertent omission please apply to the publisher for rectification.

ISBN: 978 1 4451 5654 5

Printed in China

Franklin Watts
An imprint of
Hachette Children's Group
Part of The Watts Publishing Group
Carmelite House
50 Victoria Embankment
London EC4Y 0DZ

An Hachette UK Company
www.hachette.co.uk

www.franklinwatts.co.uk